Sapphire's
Summer Disguise

UNICORN
University

#6

Sapphire's
Summer
Disguise

★ by DAISY SUNSHINE ★

illustrated by MONIQUE DONG

ALADDIN
New York London Toronto Sydney New Delhi

ALADDIN

An imprint of Simon & Schuster Children's Publishing Division

1230 Avenue of the Americas, New York, New York 10020

First Aladdin paperback edition June 2022

Text copyright © 2022 by Simon & Schuster, Inc.

Illustration copyright © 2022 by Monique Dong

Also available in an Aladdin hardcover edition.

All rights reserved, including the right of reproduction in whole or in part in any form.

ALADDIN and related logo are registered trademarks of Simon & Schuster, Inc.

For information about special discounts for bulk purchases, please contact Simon & Schuster Special Sales at 1-866-506-1949 or business@simonandschuster.com.

The Simon & Schuster Speakers Bureau can bring authors to your live event. For more information or to book an event contact the Simon & Schuster Speakers Bureau at 1-866-248-3049 or visit our website at www.simonspeakers.com.

Book designed by Laura Lyn DiSiena

The illustrations for this book were rendered digitally.

The text of this book was set in Tinos.

Manufactured in the United States of America 0422 OFF

2 4 6 8 10 9 7 5 3 1

Library of Congress Cataloging-in-Publication Data

Names: Sunshine, Daisy, author. | Dong, Monique, illustrator.

Title: Sapphire's summer disguise / by Daisy Sunshine ; illustrated by Monique Dong.

Description: First Aladdin paperback edition. | New York : Aladdin, 2022. | Series: Unicorn university | Summary: Sapphire is ready to make friends at Camp Explore, but has a hard time connecting to the other unicorn campers since they are all convinced she she is Princess Nova in disguise. Identifiers: LCCN 2021051739 (print) | LCCN 2021051740 (ebook) | ISBN 9781665901000 (paperback) | ISBN 9781665901017 (hardcover) | ISBN 9781665901024 (ebook) Subjects: CYAC: Unicorns—Fiction. | Camps—Fiction. | Identity—Fiction. Classification: LCC PZ7.1.S867 Sas 2022 (print) | LCC PZ7.1.S867 (ebook) | DDC [Fic]—dc23

LC record available at https://lccn.loc.gov/2021051739

LC ebook record available at https://lccn.loc.gov/2021051740

For lovers of sparkles, rainbows, and magic

CONTENTS

1

First Day at Camp!

Dear Sapphire,

We miss you already! Hope you're having the
best time ever. Here are a few things we
think will make you smile. Can't wait to hear
all about your camp adventures!!!
Love,
Comet, Twilight, and Shamrock

Sapphire tossed her long blue braids over her shoulder
as she read the note from her very best friends. On the table

in front of her was a big package wrapped in crinkled brown paper, waiting to be opened.

But she stopped just before tearing off the paper, her hoof hanging in midair.

It felt like someone—or something!—was watching her. The "ghost" she and her friends had met at Sapphire's seaside sleepover had turned out to be a friendly narwhal named Ned, but could the cabin at her summer camp be haunted for real?

Sapphire heard a creak and a whisper, and she looked around the small cabin to see if anyone was there. But all she could see were the wide wooden floorboards and walls made of big tree logs. There were signs that her cabinmates had already arrived, like the towel hanging from one of the hooks and the stack of magazines on the table, but she was the only unicorn in the cabin. Smiling at herself, Sapphire shrugged and brushed it off. *It's probably the wind whistling through the trees*, she thought. *Maybe I'm not used to being in the woods!*

Sapphire had just arrived at Camp Explore in the Great Green Forest of Sunshine Springs, which was far from her home by the ocean. Sapphire was used to the sounds of crashing waves and the salty air of the beach. Here the sounds of birds chirping and the smells of pine trees filled the air. It felt like she was in a different world.

Sapphire had wanted to go to Camp Explore because her hero, Amelia Hoofheart, had gone here when she'd been just a filly. Amelia Hoofheart was a famous unicorn explorer known for her brave adventures. Sapphire wanted to be a famous explorer just like her. *I might be standing just where Amelia Hoofheart once stood!* Sapphire thought. She couldn't help but do a little happy dance on her hooves.

Amelia Hoofheart had flown a hot-air balloon all over the five kingdoms. She had disappeared on her flight to visit the Arctic Foxes, and no one had seen her, or her hot-air balloon, for more than twenty years. Sapphire always hoped the explorer would turn up with a grand story to tell. And sometimes Sapphire dreamed of being the unicorn to find Amelia Hoofheart. Then she would be a famous explorer and a hero too.

A well-loved copy of Amelia Hoofheart's autobiography peeked out from Sapphire's overstuffed bag. The cover was peeling at the corners, and the pages were crinkly and brown. But Sapphire still thought the book was perfect.

She carefully pulled it out and flipped to the first chapter. She read the first lines for the one millionth time.

> *Camp Explore was the site of my first*
> *adventure. My cabinmates and I were*
> *kindred spirits and fast friends. Every day*

we would try something new. We broke swimming records and ran in the relay races. Every day was a new adventure. We loved planning and playing pranks on each other, other campers, and sometimes even the counselors.

One day one of us—we can never remember who—decided to hike to the top of Mount Cliff, so named for its high peaks and rocky terrain. It was said that no camper had made it to the top. We decided to plant our camp flag on the top so everyone would know that Camp Explore had been there first.

We woke up before sunrise, when the rest of the camp was still slumbering. We trekked up the mountainside, helping each other along the way. When we arrived,

sweaty and happy, we cheered as we pulled
out our flag to plant. But all of a sudden
there was a noise from behind us, a small
musical voice saying, "Now, just what do
you think you're doing?"

Sapphire knew the story by heart. A fairy had come to explain that lots of creatures traveled through the mountains, and many more called the top of the mountain their home. There wasn't a flag planted because the mountaintop belonged to everyone. Amelia Hoofheart said that this was when she'd first learned what it meant to be an explorer.

Sapphire loved the story for two reasons.

One, it reminded her of when she'd met Fairy Green. It was at school, at Unicorn University, and she'd helped find the fairy's lost magical dust. That day Sapphire had discovered her magical ability. It wasn't like her friends' magic—she couldn't fly or turn invisible—but Fairy Green had told her that magic came in many forms, and Sapphire's magic was her curiosity and good heart.

And two, Sapphire had always loved the phrase "kindred spirits" that Amelia Hoofheart used. Sapphire had never heard the phrase before reading this book, but she figured it meant "unicorns who felt like friends even if you had never met them before." Her friends back at Unicorn University were kindred spirits, and the four of them had been friends since their very first day at school. And now Sapphire couldn't wait to meet her cabinmates on her very first day of camp!

Sapphire smiled as she turned back to the package her friends had sent. First she pulled out a big white box tied with a yellow ribbon. The sticker on the box said "Curley's Confections." Sapphire knew this must be from Comet, who was spending the summer studying baking with her uncle Curley at his famous bakery right in Celestial City, the capital of Sunshine Springs. He baked cookies for the king and queen! Sapphire opened the box to find a pile of beautiful sugar cookies that *almost* looked too good to eat. They looked like little yellow stars, with sugar crystals blinking in the sunlight.

Munching on a cookie, next Sapphire pulled out a painting of the Crystal Library, her favorite place at Unicorn University. It looked like a glittering castle and was filled with books on every subject. Sapphire could tell that Twilight had painted this, which made it even more of a treasure.

A pair of big black sunglasses rolled out of some green tissue paper. Sapphire read the note and was surprised to discover that they were from Shamrock. He was always very studious, so she would have expected him to send a book on bugs or stars or rocks. But glamorous sunglasses? She opened his note and read, "Dear Sapphire—Don't forget to protect your eyes! You're going to be out on the lake all day swimming and high up in the mountains hiking. It's important to wear sunglasses. I've been reading about this inventor . . ." The note went on to describe the inventor of sunglasses, but Sapphire put it aside, thinking she would finish it later. She admired the big, dark glasses—and she was happy to find that they looked more like something a movie star would wear than a scientist.

Sapphire hung up Twilight's painting on the cabin wall and had that weird feeling again. Like she was being watched. She looked around and this time spotted three horns bobbing outside one of the cabin windows. Sapphire had little sisters, so she was used to being spied on. She cleared her throat. "I can see you, you know," she said, laughing. Maybe her fellow campers were playing a prank on her!

But before Sapphire could find out, she heard a whistle blow. "All campers to the mess hall steps," a voice boomed over a loudspeaker.

Not wanting to miss out on anything, Sapphire rushed toward the door, forgetting about the horns she'd seen through the window. Seeing Shamrock's sunglasses on the table, she decided to put them on before heading out, and pushed them over her nose with her hoof.

Other campers smiled at her as she joined the crowd of unicorns in front of the big wooden cabin with a wide front porch. She saw a sign swinging above the doors that read MESS HALL.

Sapphire found a place on the grass where she could

see the older unicorns lined up on the porch, as if it were a stage. Sapphire was a little shorter than most unicorns her age, so she stood apart a little, up on the hill so she could see. Most of the counselors were teenagers, and they all looked *cool* with their colorful lanyards and whistles hanging around their necks. One unicorn wore a baseball hat, one wore a bandanna, and one wore black sunglasses, kind of like Sapphire's. Sapphire instantly felt cooler and made a mental note to thank Shamrock for thinking of them, even if glamour wasn't quite what he'd had in mind.

"Welcome to the mess hall! That's what we call the dining hall here at camp. It's where we'll eat all our meals and gather at the start of each day. I know you've all met your cabinmates. . . ."

Sapphire realized that all the other campers were standing in groups. *Everyone must be standing with their cabinmates,* she thought, feeling a little worried. She hadn't even met her cabinmates yet! Now she was the only one standing alone. *Did I arrive too late?* Sapphire couldn't help but feel like she was starting off on the wrong hoof. She hoped she hadn't already messed up her chances of being the next Amelia Hoofheart.

Sapphire was surprised when the whistle blew once more, announcing the end of the welcome meeting. The counselors dismissed them and said for everyone to go back to their cabins to get unpacked. She had been so busy worrying about doing things wrong that she hadn't focused on anything the counselor was saying! Sapphire took a deep breath and hoped her cabinmates would be there when she got back. She was determined to make a good first impression.

2

First Impressions

Sapphire pushed open the wooden door of her cabin to find three unicorns looking back at her.

"Hi!" a lime-green unicorn said, stepping forward. "I'm Glimmer."

Sapphire smiled, relieved and hoping she looked friendly and kindred-spirit-like. "I'm Sapphire. It's so great to meet you. I was a little nervous at the welcome meeting. It felt like everyone was already with their cabinmates, and I was worried I'd missed my opportunity." *Oops*, the words

came tumbling out, and Sapphire wondered if they made any sense.

Glimmer just waved her hoof. "Nope! We three came early because of my aunt. She's the camp director, so we all got to ride with her this morning and scope out the camp before everyone else got here."

Sapphire blinked in surprise. "Oh—you already know each other?" She tried not to sound disappointed. She felt a little left out, being the only new one in the cabin.

"We were all cabinmates last year," the unicorn who was the color blue of a robin's egg told her. "I'm Sparkles—oooh! Are those cookies from the capital?" she asked, her voice squealing with excitement when she saw Comet's box on the table.

"Yes. My—" Sapphire started to tell her about Comet, but Glimmer interrupted.

"Of course they're from the capital, Sparkles," Glimmer said. "I *told* you so."

"Oh, have you been before?" Sapphire asked. "I've always wanted to go and see the castle library!"

Glimmer rolled her eyes. "You don't need to pretend with us. My aunt told me all about you."

Sapphire tilted her head in surprise. *Are we talking about the same thing?* she wondered. *I thought we were talking about cookies.*

"I couldn't believe it at first," the bright yellow unicorn piped in. "But it really does add up, the fancy cookies and the glamorous glasses. Not to mention the painting of the castle!" She quickly bowed to Sapphire, putting one leg out in front of her and lowering her head.

Now Sapphire was really confused. "Huh?" she asked. *Is this one of the famous pranks Amelia Hoofheart talked about?*

"So, is that like a country castle?" Sparkles asked. "I've been to the capital, so I know that's not what the main castle looks like."

"Is that where you usually spend your summers?" Glimmer asked.

The questions just kept pouring out. Sapphire felt like they were coming so fast that she didn't know which to answer first!

"Do you wear a crown?"

"Have you met other princesses?"

"Do you go to school?"

"Do you go to *princess* school?"

Luckily, Sapphire was saved by the sound of a trumpet.

"Oh, that's dinner! We don't want to be late. I happen to know they have a special dinner prepared for the first night," she said with the toss of her mane.

Sapphire watched them file out of the cabin and fell a little behind. She wondered if she had ever felt quite so confused. She didn't know what to think. *I am missing something for sure.*

Sapphire lost track of her cabinmates on the way to the mess hall. It was as if they were playing a game and Sapphire didn't know the rules. She hoped they weren't making fun of her.

As she walked, Sapphire noticed the lake across the big green lawn that sprawled out from the mess hall steps. The camp looked the way she had imagined; she just wished it could feel the way she'd imagined. *Maybe I just got off on the wrong hoof*, she decided. *I'll clear it up with my cabinmates inside.*

But when she got into the hall, her cabinmates were already huddled around a table with lots of other campers, and there didn't seem to be any room for her. With a sinking stomach, Sapphire realized she would have to eat dinner alone. Her heart pounded. Part of her wanted to run out that door and all the way back to the ocean.

You want to be brave like Amelia Hoofheart, right? So be brave! she told herself. Standing taller, she looked around for a spot where she could eat dinner. She might not have felt brave, but at least she could pretend to be.

Suddenly something bumped into Sapphire and made her wobble on her hooves! When she steadied herself, she came face-to-face with a blue unicorn with green bangs hanging over big, round glasses.

The other unicorn shook her head to straighten her glasses, which reminded Sapphire of Shamrock, whose glasses were always going askew—usually when he was explaining some fact. It made Sapphire smile wide just to think about it.

The other unicorn smiled back. "Sorry about bumping into you! I was trying to find a place to sit."

Sapphire nodded. "That's why I stopped! I was looking around too."

"I saw a spot over in the corner. Want to—um—want to . . . ?" The unicorn stumbled over her words, suddenly shy.

"Let's sit together!" Sapphire said, happy to have someone to eat dinner with after all.

They headed to the nearest bench, and soon plates full of roasted vegetables and gravy arrived in front of them.

"This looks delicious!" the other unicorn said enthusiastically. "It's so . . . messy."

Sapphire laughed and tilted her head. "I guess so. . . . Kinda just feels like regular old dinner to me."

"I'm Nellie, by the way," the other unicorn said.

"I'm Sapphire!" she told her in the middle of a big bite of vegetables. "It's nice to meet you," she added after swallowing.

"You too," Nellie said. "Truthfully, I've been nervous about sitting alone and not meeting any kindred spirits."

Sapphire looked up with a start. "Have you read Amelia Hoofheart's autobiography?" she asked with a squeal.

"Only one million times!" Nellie said.

The two blue unicorns spent the rest of the dinner talking about adventures and Amelia Hoofheart, and where she might have been right then. As they made their way through cream pies for dessert, Sapphire was feeling kingdoms better about camp.

After dinner Sapphire and Nellie parted, with promises to find each other the next morning. Back at Sapphire's cabin, her strange cabinmates were still at dinner, so Sapphire pulled out her postcards to write notes to her friends, to thank them for the welcome gifts and tell them all about her first day.

Sapphire went to bed with hopes that the next day would not be quite as strange as today.

3

Day Two at Camp Explore

Dear Sapphire,

I looked up the coordinates of your
camp, and you should be able to see
the Dragon Claw Constellation. You are
in one of the only places in Sunshine
Springs where you can see it!

Shamrock

Sapphire woke up with a start. She'd been having a
dream that she couldn't quite remember, and as she blinked

away the sleepiness, she noticed that the cabin was oddly quiet. No hooves scraping, or snoring, or sleepy neighs . . . *Oh no!* Sapphire realized with a sinking heart. *I must have slept through the morning trumpet.* Her grumbling stomach reminded her of just why this was such a problem. She'd missed breakfast!

Feeling grumpy, Sapphire pushed open her stall door and headed to the mess hall, hoping there were some scraps left over. She could see happy campers hanging outside their cabins and lounging on the grass with smiles on their faces. She groaned. Why did it feel like she was so bad at camp?

The big dining room was completely empty, just rows and rows of long clean tables and not a camper in sight. Luckily, there was a big bowl of apples and a basket of muffins on the counter with a note that read "For late sleepers. ☺" Sapphire munched on a few apples and muffins, and soon felt much better. Being hungry always made her grumpy, she remembered. As she brushed off the crumbs, a trumpet blared, followed by an announcement calling all the campers to the front of the mess hall.

Sapphire rushed to meet up with the rest of the camp. But when she pushed the doors open, she found herself on the porch staring at the whole camp on the lawn! And they were all staring at *her*. Sapphire blushed and stumbled down the steps, feeling so embarrassed that she wished she could go hide in the woods. Instead she found a space on the lawn and looked at her hooves.

"It's the first full day of camp!" one of the counselors yelled into a megaphone. Her voice was bubbly and happy. Without even looking at the counselor, Sapphire could tell she was smiling. "You and your cabinmates will find your first activity listed on the chalkboard behind me." The unicorn pointed with her horn to the big green board. White lines of chalk outlined a chart with activities listed on the top; Sapphire could see swimming, hiking, art class, and more. And then cabin numbers were listed underneath.

Sapphire realized that she would be with her cabin-mates for *all* the activities during the day. She squared her shoulders and promised herself that she would clear the air and try to get on the same page as them. Putting on a big, brave smile, she looked around and tried to find Glimmer or Sparkles. That was when she saw the bright yellow unicorn from the day before wave her over. *Time to try this again.*

Sapphire walked over, thinking of a speech to say when she got there. But the yellow unicorn had a speech prepared too. "Hi! I realized I never told you my name yesterday," the yellow unicorn said. "I've been totally kicking myself since. And then you were asleep when we got back to the cabin, and then you slept through the morning bugle this morning. . . . You must have been tired! Did you have to travel a long way to get to camp?" Her speech came out in a rush, and when she'd finished, she had to stop to take a breath.

Sapphire smiled. This unicorn might have been talking quickly, but at least Sapphire understood what she was talking about! "I came all the way from the ocean. But, um, you never did tell me your name."

"I'm Ray!" She smiled, and little dimples popped out in her cheeks.

"Nice to meet you," Sapphire said. "I'm Sapphire."

Ray was about to say something, when Glimmer and Sparkles walked over.

"You guys!" Glimmer called out, sounding a little annoyed. "We're supposed to be heading to swimming class. Let's go!"

Ray and Sapphire followed behind Glimmer and Sparkles as they made their way to the lake.

"So, have you met Prince Ned?" asked Ray.

Sapphire groaned. "Okay, you guys have to drop this prank. Or at least tell me what's going on!"

Ray, Sparkles, and Glimmer all looked at each other. It was as if they were having a silent conversation that they didn't want Sapphire to know about.

"Did I do something wrong?" Sapphire asked. "Did I miss something?"

Sparkles and Ray pushed Glimmer ahead, as if nominating her to speak.

Glimmer stepped forward and cleared her throat. "No, you're actually, surprisingly, more normal than we thought you'd be!"

Sapphire didn't know what that meant. What had they heard about her? "Umm—"

Glimmer kept going. "But remember how my aunt is the director? Well, she let it slip that Princess Luna would be at camp. And so of course we figured out that you're her in disguise!"

"Your mane is different," Sparkles said, "but you look just like you do in pictures!" She pulled a magazine out of her bag. Princess Luna stared out from the cover.

Sapphire could only laugh. "I'm not Princess Luna!" she said. "You've made a huge mistake!"

"You're really trying to tell us this isn't you?" Ray asked, pointing to Sparkles's magazine with her horn.

Sapphire studied the image. A blue unicorn with blue eyes and big wavy curls stared back at her. The unicorn had a glittering crown on top of her head and was smiling with confidence. Sapphire couldn't believe that these unicorns thought this glamorous, royal unicorn looked like regular old Sapphire!

When she looked up at her cabinmates, she could see them all staring at her with wide-eyed looks, as if she—Sapphire—were so special that she deserved to be on the cover of a magazine. Her smile fell as she realized she was only going to disappoint them.

I'm not magical or royal, Sapphire thought. That's why Sapphire loved Amelia Hoofheart so much. Amelia hadn't used magic to travel the five kingdoms. She'd traveled using her bravery and smarts. Sapphire thought maybe someday she could be on the cover of a magazine, but right now she was just another camper. She worried what her cabinmates would say when they realized that.

"I'm sorry to disappoint you guys. I'm just a normal unicorn." Sapphire hoped they would still want to be her friend anyway.

"Yeah, sure. Let's not talk about princess stuff, okay?" Glimmer said with a wink. "We'll all be regular old unicorns. Together."

Sapphire smiled at her with relief. She didn't want them to be upset because she wasn't who they'd expected. It would have been a lot cooler to cabin with a princess than with just another camper, after all. But the three cabinmates still smiled at her and wanted to walk with her. Sapphire was feeling like they might be kindred spirits after all.

Walking side by side, the unicorns made their way to the lake, which was filled with unicorns splashing and laughing. Sapphire smiled, happy to be leaving the misunderstanding behind her, and ran in to join the fun.

4

Just Keep Swimming

Dear Sapphire,

It's a little weird being back at home after
so many months at Unicorn University. Home
feels smaller. Or maybe I feel bigger?

I'm sorry camp got off to a rocky start, but
I know you'll turn it around. If anyone knows
how to have a grand adventure, it's you.

Love,

Twilight

As the day went on, Sapphire learned that she and Glimmer had not been speaking the same language after all. Now the whole camp thought Sapphire was a princess!

She realized something was wrong when she was swimming in the lake. At first she felt like she was back at home, splashing confidently through the cool, fresh water. But soon she had that prickly sense on the back of her neck again. It felt like ghosts—a lot of ghosts—were watching her.

After getting out of the water, Sapphire paused on the beach and shook herself dry. But she couldn't shake the feeling that people were whispering about her.

She didn't have time to worry about it for long, though, because soon a counselor blew a whistle to get the campers' attention.

"Time for lunch!" she called out. She pointed her horn to the baskets of carrots and jam sandwiches. The hungry unicorns rushed over, and soon the baskets were empty.

The counselor blew the whistle again. "Now it's time to get ready for relay races! Each cabin will be a team. First section is 'the swamp crawl,' where each camper will have to make their way through the muddy, sticky, swampy part of the lake to get to their cabinmate waiting in the low water."

All the campers started laughing and erupted into a chorus of "Eww!" and "Not me! No way!"

The counselor just chuckled and kept going. "The next unicorn will have to swim through the maze of buoys in the lake to reach the shore and pass the flag to their cabinmate waiting on the sand."

The crowd only mumbled slightly. Swimming through the lake didn't seem so hard.

"The unicorn on the beach will have to build a sandcastle before passing the flag to the fourth cabinmate for the final part of the race. The last unicorn will have to gallop to the end of the dock and ring the bell. The first team to ring the bell wins an ice cream party at their cabin tonight!"

All the campers cheered and then gathered with their groups to talk about strategy.

"I'm on my cross-country team at school, so I should be the one to ring the bell," Glimmer said first.

"Well, I'm not going into that swamp!" Sparkles said. "Think of what it will do to my hooficure! But I am good at building sandcastles, so I can do that."

"Oh yuck," Ray whined. "I don't want to go into the swamp either."

Sapphire chuckled. "I'll go into the swamp! I don't mind." She expected the other unicorns to be happy, but instead they looked worried.

"No, no, it's fine. I can do it," Ray said quickly.

Sapphire was about to tell her not to worry, but a counselor jumped in. "I think that's a good idea, Ray. Um, why don't you do the swimming part, Your High—I mean, um, Sapphire." The counselor blushed and moved away.

Sapphire's jaw dropped. Even the counselors thought she was a princess! She was speechless and fuming mad. Even if she had been a princess, she should have been able to do what she wanted! But before she could cause a fuss, the whistle blew as the signal to start the race. Ray took a deep breath and ran bravely into the swamp.

Unfortunately, Ray was quickly left behind by the other campers. She kept saying "Ew, ew, ew" and tried to jump from rock to rock. But she just ended up falling more than anything else. By the time she got to Sapphire in the water, the other teams were already making sandcastles. Sapphire swam as fast as she could, and Glimmer really was a fast runner, but their team still came in dead last.

Sapphire loved games. She was good at them, and she *really* loved winning. And if her teammates had let her go into the swamp, they probably would have won. *Ugh*, Sapphire thought. *This princess thing is ruining everything.*

When the whistle blew for free swim, Sapphire jumped back into the water, hoping to cool herself off. *I just want to swim away from all this.*

She opened her eyes underwater to see small silver fish swimming around her hooves. Then she spotted a slowly swimming turtle in the distance. That made her feel better. Nature was awesome!

But when Sapphire reemerged into the world, she accidently bumped into another unicorn, a blue one with green bangs and big green glasses.

"We meet again!" Nellie said. It was the unicorn

Sapphire had had dinner with! Sapphire's conversation with Nellie had been the only normal one she'd had since she'd arrived at camp. She hoped Nellie hadn't heard the rumor that Sapphire was a princess. . . .

"I've had art class all morning," Nellie told her as they treaded water out in the lake. "But I came to swim right after! I'm jealous you had swimming this morning."

Sapphire nodded. "It is nice. The water's perfect, and it's much different from swimming in the ocean back home. There's no waves or salty air. You would think that that's what is making me homesick, but really it's the other campers." *Oops.* Sapphire hadn't meant to let all that out. Somehow Nellie made her feel like she was with a good friend. *I wonder if that's what makes a kindred spirit,* Sapphire thought.

Sapphire looked back to shore and saw Glimmer and her other cabinmates on the sandy beach. She wanted to get as far away from them as possible.

"Race to the island?" Sapphire asked, pointing to a tiny cluster of trees in the middle of the lake.

Nellie's eyes lit up. "Wow! Cool! Ready, set . . . go!"

The two blue unicorns giggled and splashed all the way to the island and were panting as they pulled themselves onto the tiny floating forest. Standing together, they looked back at camp and all the unicorns still splashing near the shore.

"Wow, it feels so far away," Nellie said, still a little out of breath. "Like we've traveled somewhere new."

Sapphire sighed happily. It felt good to swim away from all the stares for a minute. She felt like she was finally allowed to take off the princess mask.

"Did you know that Amelia Hoofheart would wear disguises so people wouldn't recognize her?" Nellie asked.

Sapphire wondered if Nellie had the magical ability to read minds. "I never realized how hard it must have been for her, until today," she admitted.

"What do you mean?" Nellie asked.

Sapphire shifted on her hooves. She knew she needed to tell someone about this princess rumor, even if it was the last thing she felt like talking about. That was one lesson she'd learned from her friends at Unicorn University—it's always best to talk out your problems. "Well, my cabinmates think I'm someone I'm not. And I can't seem to convince them that I'm regular old me."

"Who do they think you are?" Nellie asked.

"Princess Luna!" Sapphire said, laughing. "It's ridiculous."

Nellie looked at her and squinted. "I can see it, actually!"

Sapphire shook her head so hard that her braids whipped back and forth. "I mean, it's actually really nice if you think about it. They think boring old me is a royal princess? I don't even have a magical ability! How could I be the princess of magical unicorns?" Sapphire blew out her lips. "But what if Princess Luna really is here at camp, and she finds out people think I'm her? I don't want the royal family to be mad at me!"

Nellie smiled. "Don't worry, they wouldn't be."

Sapphire laughed. "You don't know that!"

Nellie took a deep breath. "Can you keep a secret?" She looked off into the distance as if she were trying to see something far away.

Sapphire raised her eyebrows. She had no idea what Nellie was going to say. But Sapphire really could keep a secret. "Totally!"

Nellie smiled and pulled Sapphire farther into the forest, where they could no longer see the rest of the camp. She took off her green curls, which turned out to be a wig, revealing blue bouncing curls underneath. Then she peered over her green glasses. "Recognize me?" she asked.

Sapphire gasped. "Princess Luna?!" She was stunned. A real princess? She didn't know what to say.

Suddenly she understood better why her cabinmates had

been so weird. Being in front of a real royal was like something out of a fairy tale. All Sapphire could do was stare.

"It's a disguise," Nellie said. "Amelia Hoofheart inspired me."

Sapphire tried to find her words. It was a strange feeling because she usually had an opinion or thought about everything!

"Do you believe me?" Nellie asked. She bit her bottom lip and shuffled on her hooves.

Sapphire could understand—Nellie had just revealed a huge secret. And she needed a good friend right now to tell her it was okay. Sapphire finally found her voice. "Of course I believe you!" Sapphire said. "I guess I'm a little stunned. I've been so worried about being mistaken for a princess that . . . I totally missed a real princess right in front of me."

"Well, that's kind of what the disguise was for," Nellie said, chuckling. "But I'm worried my secret won't stay a secret for too long," she continued. "Whenever I go out in disguise, people always figure it out. I'm no Amelia Hoofheart, really."

Sapphire shook her head. "No way! You have the whole camp fooled. It's amazing."

Nellie beamed. "I planned it all out myself. I based it on one of Amelia's disguises, actually. There's a big book of photos of her in the royal library."

Sapphire's eyes widened at the idea of the royal library. She had only heard stories of the place that held the royal family's own personal collection of books.

"I've always wanted to see the royal library!" Sapphire squeaked. "Is it like the pictures? Are there really books of every size? I heard there was one that was bigger than a dragon and another that was smaller than a fairy. Are there really maps of every part of the five kingdoms? And . . ." Sapphire trailed off, realizing she was acting totally uncool. She was acting like her cabinmates! And she remembered how weird that had felt. "Oh—I'm sorry. I'm talking too much!"

Nellie smiled, clearly more used to questions like this than Sapphire had been. "We don't have books the size of dragons, but there is a collection of old maps that's a little bigger than me. You should come to the capital sometime to see!"

Sapphire's breath caught in her throat. "That would be a great adventure!"

Sapphire and Nellie smiled at each other, as if they both could tell this was the start of a great friendship. *Kindred spirits*, Sapphire thought.

"So," Sapphire said. "Now that I know your real name, what should I call you?"

"Can we stick with 'Nellie' this week?" she asked with a smile. "It's a nickname my grandma gave me. I don't really want to be Princess Luna right now. I just want to try to be normal."

"Totally," Sapphire said. "I've only had one day of being a princess, and it's not as fun as I thought it would be."

Nellie nodded, her curls bouncing around her shoulders. "Everyone always thinks they know what's best for you."

"Exactly!" Sapphire said. "They wouldn't let me run in the swamp, and then my team lost the relay race!"

Nellie laughed. "I'm not sure most unicorns *want* to run in a swamp, but I know what you mean. Unicorns always expect you to be so proper, and sometimes you just want to let loose! And I feel like I never get to really know any-one because everyone thinks they already know me." Nellie paused and looked down. "Does that make sense?"

"It does," Sapphire told her. "Since everyone thought I was you, it's been kind of lonely, actually. It's made me miss my four best friends."

Nellie sighed. "I've never had a real friend before."

Sapphire looked up with a start. Nellie was so nice and fun! She should have had lots of friends. If only unicorns would see her as Nellie and not as Princess Luna. Sapphire chewed her bottom lip, wishing she could help. After all, she had decided to use her magical power to be brave and help people. How could she help Princess Luna feel like a normal unicorn?

Then an idea struck her like a bolt of lightning. She gave Nellie a look that her friends at Unicorn University always called her Adventure Look.

Nellie must have seen something in Sapphire's eyes,

because she asked, "What's up? What are you thinking?"

"I think I have an idea," Sapphire told her. "A way for you to keep being Nellie this week—and not worry about people figuring out your disguise."

"How?" Nellie asked.

"If I'm going to be a great explorer like Amelia Hoofheart, I should learn the art of disguise, don't you think?"

5

The Art of Disguise

To S,

Did the campers like my cookies? I hear
they're Princess Luna's favorite. I wonder
if I'll see her while I'm in the capital. . . .
There's so much I have to tell you, but
I'm baking constantly and there's no time
to write. ☹
Miss you lots and lots and lots.
XOXO,
Comet

Sapphire and Nellie swam back to shore, plotting and planning all the while.

Sapphire would be the decoy princess, never quite saying she was a princess, but not trying to prove she wasn't, either. It would make the campers focus on Sapphire and never realize Nellie was the real princess.

"Thanks again, Sapphire," Nellie said as they swam. "This is the nicest thing anyone has ever done for me, and . . . well, I'm a princess, so people do nice things for me all the time."

Sapphire smiled, her heart soaring in her chest. This week might have started off not so great, but now she was beginning a great adventure! She was helping a princess with a secret mission. Sapphire felt like she was Amelia Hoofheart.

The lake was quiet again as the two unicorns swam back to shore. The shouts and giggles of splashing campers were gone, and the sun was starting to disappear behind the mountains.

The unicorns ran up onto the shore and shook the water off to get dry.

"Let's head to our cabins for our towels and sweatshirts," Sapphire suggested. The air was cooling down, without the sun high in the sky. She shivered as the wind blew.

Nellie nodded, and together they headed in the direction of the cabins. Sapphire couldn't see any campers around, and she thought it was safe to keep talking about their super-secret plan. "Anything I should know about you? I don't really read the magazines, so I don't know very much."

Nellie laughed. "Most of what's in the magazines isn't true anyway! But okay, here are some things: I love Amelia Hoofheart, which you already know. I love to swim, and you already know that, too. Hmmm . . . I live in the capital mostly, except when we go on vacations or to visit other royal families."

Other royal families! Sapphire tried to act normal and

not totally starstruck. "I didn't know there was a unicorn school in the capital," she said finally.

Nellie shook her head. "There's not. I just have tutors. That's why I wanted to go to camp!"

Sapphire loved Unicorn University, she couldn't imagine

not being able to go to the beautiful fields and learn from all her teachers. Now she felt doubly happy that she was helping Nellie with her secret mission.

Nellie and Sapphire each ran to her own cabin to grab a big, cozy sweatshirt. They met each other back on the lawn, but still there wasn't another unicorn in sight. It was like the whole camp had disappeared. Sapphire could only hear a bird hooting in the distance. "Where is everyone?" she wondered aloud.

Nellie's eyes went wide, as if remembering something important. "Dinner!" she said.

"Did we miss it?" Sapphire worried.

They broke into a gallop and ran to the mess hall.

Luckily, the two unicorns arrived with dinner still in full swing. All the noise from camp was now packed into the long wooden room.

Sounds of hooves scraping against the floor and plates clattering together filled the air.

"Nellie! Over here!" a group of unicorns called from one side of the room.

"Princess! I mean, um, Sapphire!" Glimmer called from the other side.

"You ready?" Nellie asked.

"Let's do this!" Sapphire said.

And with a quick horn tap, the two unicorns went their separate ways.

6

What Would Amelia Hoofheart Do?

Sapphire,

Astronomy camp is amazing, but it's hard staying up so late. I love looking at the stars, but I like sleeping too. . . . I wish I could be in two places at once! Have you had any adventures yet?

Shamrock

Sapphire woke up feeling refreshed. She'd been so tired when she'd gone to bed the night before that she'd fallen asleep as soon as her head had hit the pillow. *Must be all the swimming*, she thought.

Sapphire had just started her morning stretches when she heard Glimmer's voice call out, "Princess! Time for breakfast!"

Sapphire was about to correct Glimmer when she remembered the plan. For a moment she thought Nellie revealing herself as Princess Luna had been a dream. *Today will be the real test for my disguise.*

"No maids to help this morning," Sparkles added from across the cabin, teasing.

"I don't have any maids," Sapphire told them. "But I do have a personal chef." They didn't have to know that she meant her best friend Comet, and she was more of a baker than a chef.

With a dramatic mane flip, Sapphire walked out of the cabin for breakfast. Her three cabinmates followed close behind, asking her questions and giggling.

At breakfast it was clear that word about Princess Luna had spread throughout the camp. Everyone came by Sapphire's table to say hello and compliment her mane style. Unicorns kept asking her if she needed anything. Sapphire had to admit, it was kind of fun being the center of atten-tion. At least it was better than feeling as alone as she had on that first night. Things had gone from her worrying that no one wanted to sit with her at dinner to there not being enough room for all the unicorns who wanted to sit with her at breakfast!

As breakfast calmed down, a coun-selor walked to the front of the room and whistled to get their attention, and after a few moments all the morning chatter trickled to a stop. The counselor's red mane was in two long braids framing her face, and she wore a colorful bead necklace around her neck.

"Morning, campers!" she yelled in a booming voice. "I want to remind you all of our camp tradition! At the end of camp week, we host an all-camp talent show. When I was a camper, I showed off my juggling skills. Some campers like to sing, and others like to perform a skit. Feel free to do whatever you want! This is the time to show your new friends what you can do! Sign up by the end of the day to make sure you have a spot on this list."

After this announcement, what started as whispers at the tables turned into full-on conversations and yelling. Everyone wanted to know who was signing up and what they were going to do. Sapphire could feel the energy and excitement buzzing around the room, but she quickly decided not to sign up. *I'm already putting on the biggest performance of my life*, she thought as she listened to her cabinmates talk.

The counselor with the braids whistled again to call the campers back to order. "I like to see the enthusiasm! But it's time for activities. Off you go!"

With that, everyone pushed back from the tables to set out for their camp activities. Sapphire was excited that they had Wilderness Skills class first, where she'd learn how to survive in the woods. As an explorer, survival was one of the most important skills.

Sapphire joined the river of campers leaving the mess hall and started following the signs for Wilderness Skills. Glimmer, Sparkles, and Ray caught up with her on the way.

"I can't wait to hear you sing!" Ray said as she fell into step with Sapphire.

"Huh?" Sapphire asked.

"I think Ray just means that everyone knows how well you can sing," Sparkles said. "I mean, everyone in Sunshine Springs knows how good a singer Princess Luna is."

Sapphire gulped. She and Nellie had gone over details about Nellie's life, but she didn't remember anything about singing!

"I remember reading about how you sang at the king's birthday party," Ray added.

Sapphire did love to sing, but she'd never been able to sing in front of crowds or strangers. Performing in front of the whole camp? That was a nightmare.

But then a little voice in her head said, *What would Amelia Hoofheart do?*

Sapphire stopped to think. *Amelia Hoofheart would face her fears*, Sapphire decided. *And so would a princess.*

Sapphire put on a big smile, hoping she looked more confident than she felt. "Of *course* I'll be singing in the talent show!"

Sparkles and Ray cheered as they started walking again. But when Sapphire looked over to Glimmer, she saw an odd look on the green unicorn's face. Her eyebrows were scrunched as if she were thinking about something. Sapphire shrugged. Glimmer was just a hard unicorn to figure out, she thought.

7

Wilderness Skills

Dear Sapphire,

I heard from Comet today. Sounds like the
capital is wonderful. But I would worry
about being around so many unicorns. Do
you think we'll get to go someday?

Love,

Twilight

Sapphire and her cabinmates followed the wooden signs.

Most of the camp activities happened close to the mess hall

and had big bright banners to direct campers, but to get to Wilderness Skills class, campers had to hike a narrow path through the woods.

It was quiet away from the noise of camp, and Sapphire and her cabinmates were soon too out of breath from the hike to do much talking. Sapphire breathed deeply. She had been pretending to be a princess for only a morning, but she was exhausted already. She hoped she could keep it up for the rest of the week. There was still the rest of the day and then two more days after that! She didn't want to let Princess Luna—or Amelia Hoofheart—down.

All of a sudden the unicorns found themselves at a clearing in the woods. There were ropes hanging from trees, and there was a little log cabin, but there was no counselor in sight. The four looked around and then at each other, wondering what to do next.

"Should we knock?" Glimmer asked, pointing to the door with her horn.

Just then the sun went behind a cloud, making the woods feel much darker and full of shadows. The wind whistled through the trees. Sapphire shivered, feeling like she'd just walked into a scary story.

Okay, it's a little scary being without a counselor in the woods, Sapphire thought. *But we're just being silly. What's scary about knocking on a door?*

Feeling brave, and a little proud of herself, Sapphire walked toward the door.

"No!" Ray screeched from behind her. "A princess probably shouldn't, like, knock on doors herself, right? She should be announced?"

Sapphire couldn't help but roll her eyes. She'd been hoping her cabinmates would feel impressed by her bravery— but it looked like the princess thing would be getting in the way of her plans . . . again!

"A princess?" a voice asked from the woods.

All four unicorns whipped around to face the voice.

A super-tall, long-maned unicorn emerged from the trees. Their coat was brown, the long mane tangled with green leaves, and their horn was covered in mud. They looked more like a creature of the woods than a unicorn!

The unicorn lumbered out and chuckled. "Look at your faces! I must look pretty scary." They chuckled again. "Don't worry! I'm your Wilderness Skills instructor. You can call me Tiny."

Now it was Sapphire's turn to chuckle. This unicorn was anything but tiny.

"I'm Sapphire," she told them. With Tiny's big smile and soft voice, she knew there was nothing to be afraid of. "And this is Glimmer, Sparkles, and Ray." Each unicorn waved her horn as Sapphire said her name.

"Nice to meet you, campers," Tiny said. "Okay, today we're learning about knots. Useful things, knots are. You can tie packs onto your back with 'em, you can put up a tent, and even go fishing! All with the right knots."

Sapphire nodded. Having grown up by the ocean, she knew a lot about knots. Her uncle Sea Star had a boat, and he had taught her how to tie nets for fish and tie up sails in the wind—usually while telling fantastical stories he had heard from other sailors.

Tiny had set out a rope on the ground for each of them and showed them how to tie different knots with a well-worn rope. Tiny used their horn and hooves to loop the rope into different shapes.

Sapphire finished hers the fastest. She knew most of the knots already, and the new knots were only a little different from the ones she was used to.

"Well done, Sapphire!" Tiny called out. "I think you're in the running for best camp knot tier."

"Thanks. My—" Sapphire stopped short before telling Tiny about her uncle Sea Star. She was supposed to be a prin-cess, she remembered, and she guessed princesses did not help any sailors fish off boats with nets. She bit her bottom lip, trying to think of what to say now that four pairs of eyes were staring at her. "My favorite book is Amelia Hoofheart's autobiography—I've read it so many times that I can practically remember every word. And she talks all about knots." Sapphire sighed. That was true, but it felt wrong not to tell Tiny the real reason why she was so good at knots. It felt like she was lying.

"Amelia Hoofheart was a great unicorn," Tiny said, and nodded. "You know, my father knew her when she was at camp. He taught Wilderness Skills too."

Sapphire looked up with awe. Suddenly Tiny seemed a lot more glamorous, even when covered in leaves and mud.

"What did your dad say about her?" Sapphire asked. "Was she . . . ?" Sapphire couldn't think of the right word. How would you describe the greatest explorer of all time?

But before Tiny could reply, a horn blew in the distance. Sapphire was amazed that the sound could reach them all the way up where they were.

"We'll have to pick this up later, Sapphire," Tiny told her. "It's already time for lunch! But I will say this, Dad always said she was just like you would expect—brave and kind."

Sapphire smiled as she walked away from Tiny. She wanted to be brave and kind too.

Sapphire, Sparkles, Glimmer, and Ray hurried down the trail back toward camp. They were far away and didn't want to miss lunch. All the hiking and wilderness skills had made their bellies grumble.

Luckily, the way down was much faster than the way up, and the four unicorns soon found themselves at a long wooden table in the mess hall with a big pile of food in front of each of them.

They ate happily without saying much, the now familiar sounds of the campers in the dining hall filling their ears. Sapphire kept thinking about what Tiny had said about Amelia Hoofheart. She hoped that by helping Princess Luna she was being brave and kind.

Two unicorns came up to their table as Sapphire took a big bite of pie. They whispered shyly to each other, each trying to nudge the other one closer to Sapphire.

Sapphire smiled at them and figured they were there to talk to the camp princess. "Hi!" she said.

"Hi!" the unicorns said back to her in unison. "Um, that's all we wanted to say. And—um—this is, like, the coolest thing to happen at camp."

Sapphire didn't quite know what to say. She was only pretending to be a princess. She wondered how cool they would think that was. Sapphire turned back to her pie, this time wondering how brave and kind it was to pretend to be something you weren't.

Glimmer looked over at Sapphire from across the table. There was a certain squint in Glimmer's eye, and Sapphire didn't know what it meant.

"So . . . Sapphire?" Glimmer's voice went up just a little when she said her name. "Are you going to sing the same song at the talent show that you sang at your dad's birthday?"

Sapphire gulped. She had no idea what song Nellie had sung! She chewed on a mouthful of pie slowly, trying to think of the right thing to say.

Luckily, Ray laughed, breaking the silence. "Why would she sing the Sunshine Springs song? That would be so boring."

Sapphire smiled, happy not to have to think of an answer. For some reason Glimmer frowned at Ray.

"Maybe I'll sing one of the camp songs," Sapphire suggested. Campers were always singing silly songs—you could usually hear them on your way to activities. The songs rhymed and were easy to join in on. Sapphire loved hearing the campers sing all around camp. It made her feel right at home. She liked to sing with her mom and her sisters.

"That's a fun idea," Sparkles said. "Let me know if you want me to teach you any. I know most of them. But

Glimmer knows them all, of course. She usually sings one at the talent show, actually."

"Oh really?" Sapphire asked. "Which one were you thinking of singing?"

"I'm not sure yet," Glimmer said. "You know what . . . ? We should do a duet!"

Sapphire smiled. A duet would be way easier than being alone onstage. "Yes!" she agreed happily. "I would love that."

"Should we work on the song now?" Glimmer asked. "We have free time until dinner."

"I want to write a few postcards first," Sapphire said. "Can you meet me after that?"

Glimmer nodded. "I'll meet up with you at the cabin."

Sapphire pushed away from the table. She walked out of the hall, looking forward to a moment alone. She loved camp, but it was tiring, always worrying about playing a role. She just wanted to spend a little time writing to the people who knew her best.

Sapphire found a quiet picnic table by the lake and pulled out her camp postcards. One side was blank, and the other said "Greetings from Camp Explore!" and there was a little compass illustration.

She wrote to her friends, telling them about her secret princess mission and asking each of them for advice. None of them had ever pretended to be a princess before, but she still hoped they could help her feel better about it all. Sapphire thought back to the unicorns at lunch. Would the whole camp be mad at her if they found out the truth?

Sapphire walked over to the mailbox and dropped the postcards in. Soon the mail pixies would pick up her postcards and zip them off to her friends across Sunshine Springs. Sapphire hoped the pixies would zip back soon with helpful advice.

After taking a deep breath and standing up straight, Sapphire headed to the cabin to meet up with Glimmer. Hooves crossed her voice was good enough to pass for Nellie's!

8

Keeping Secrets

Dear Saph (or should I say "PRINCESS"!),

I can't believe you met Princess Luna!!! Should
I bake her some cookies? I'm sure you're the
perfect princess and no one will find out.

You're on a secret mission. But maybe you'll
feel better if you talk to the real princess?

She can probably help with the talent show!

Love you lots and lots and lots,

Comet (I hope you still remember me now that
you're royal.)

The next morning Sapphire woke up early to find a postcard from Comet already slipped under her stall door. The pixies had worked quickly! Sapphire read her note and smiled. Comet was right. Sapphire should just talk to Nellie. The princess would know how to handle the talent show.

Her cabinmates were still asleep as Sapphire quietly slipped out of the cabin and walked over to Nellie's cabin. Sapphire remembered where her stall was, since she had seen Nellie go in to get her sweatshirt the other night.

Standing outside her window, Sapphire whispered, "Nellie! Nellie! Are you awake?"

After Sapphire tried a few more times, a sleepy Princess Luna popped up at the window. "I am now!" She smiled. "I'll be right out."

Sapphire and Nellie walked along the lake's shore. Everything was peaceful and quiet, and it felt like the whole world was just waking up. Sapphire told Nellie how she was supposed to sing a duet with Glimmer at the talent show—and how she worried the whole camp would realize she was a big pretender.

"Glimmer and I met up last night to talk about our duet," Sapphire said. "Luckily, she didn't ask too many questions. She basically told me what we're doing." Sapphire

shrugged. "We're singing a camp song, and she's teaching me this dance. Hopefully you're not known for being a good dancer, because I have all left hooves."

Nellie laughed. "Don't worry, I'm not a good dancer either."

Sapphire smiled. "Oh good! Well, um, are you okay with all this?"

"Of course!" Nellie said. "But are you okay with it? You seem kinda nervous."

"Well, I've never sung in front of a crowd, and also I'm nervous about letting you down. And um . . . I'm nervous about the whole camp finding out I've been pretending to be a princess." Sapphire looked up with tears in her eyes. She had been trying to keep it all together, but she just felt too overwhelmed to pretend anymore.

Nellie took a moment before responding. She tilted her head and looked off into the distance. Sapphire guessed this was Nellie's thinking face, and Sapphire bit her tongue while she waited for the princess to respond.

"Playing a role can be super hard," Nellie said softly. "Trust me, I know. But performing in front of a big crowd can be really fun. It's an amazing feeling, having a crowd cheer for you."

"But what if they hate it?" Sapphire said.

Nellie's thinking face came back before her eyes lit up with an idea. "Well, if they hate it, they'll think it was me! So you don't have to worry."

Sapphire wasn't sure that made too much sense. She would still be the one on the stage, wouldn't she? But still, she'd promised herself she would be brave, hadn't she?

"Thanks for helping keep my secret," Nellie said. "I get to be normal because of you."

Sapphire shook her head, her long braids rustling a little with the motion. "I'm glad to help you, but I'm worried we went about this all wrong. It feels like we're just lying to everyone."

Nellie paused a moment before she spoke. "Technically, the campers decided you were the princess, remember? You haven't lied to anyone."

Sapphire nodded slowly. "I guess that makes sense. It just doesn't always feel right. And I think maybe you could have convinced people to treat you like a regular camper anyway. My cabinmates were acting so weird at first, but now we're getting along like normal. I think it takes a little time to let people get to know you."

"Oh, Sapphire, please don't back out now!" Nellie said. She looked at Sapphire with pleading eyes. "These last few days have been the best of my whole life. I feel like I'm finally learning what it's like to be normal."

Sapphire's heart broke to see Nellie's face like that. "Oh, okay! What's one more day, anyway?"

The time at camp had flown by. Tonight would be the last night, and tomorrow everyone would go home. Sapphire could pretend for just a little bit longer. Nellie seemed so happy, and Sapphire was happy she could help her new friend.

Sapphire and Nellie kept walking through the woods as the sun came up. Sapphire had come to love the smells and sounds of the forest. They were different from the sounds and smells of her home by the ocean and the sounds of the fields at school, but they were just as peaceful. She loved to go on long walks through the trees and breathe in the forest air.

The two friends talked about camp things for the rest of the hike. *Not like princesses, just like two campers*, Sapphire thought.

Sapphire and Nellie made it back to the mess hall just in time for the morning bugle, and Sapphire finally felt like she was in step with the rest of the camp.

"See you at the talent show tonight," Nellie said as the two unicorns pushed through the doors, and she gave Sapphire a gentle nudge of encouragement. "I can't wait to hear you sing!"

Sapphire blushed. She couldn't believe she would be singing in front of a princess tonight. "Thank you," Sapphire said with a smile.

Looking around at the room full of campers, Sapphire felt like her stomach had been filled up with dancing beans. She was nervous, but something about Nellie's confidence in her made her feel braver. It felt good to have a friend.

Sapphire found her cabinmates and grabbed a muffin.

"Finally!" Glimmer grumbled.

Sparkles and Ray looked at each other, smiling.

"Huh?" Sapphire asked. "Did I miss something?"

"Ugh!" Glimmer grumbled even more. "The talent show, of course."

Sapphire nodded. "I know. I'm nervous too!"

"Not nervous. I'm annoyed," Glimmer went on. "We have to practice the routine so everything is perfect! I don't care if you're a princess. I like to win."

"Hey, I like to win too!" Now Sapphire was starting to get annoyed.

"Well, glad to hear it," Glimmer said, sounding a little less grumbly. "There are no activities today, so we can practice all we want."

"Great! I would love to swim before that, though. Anyone in?" Sapphire looked over at Ray and Sparkles, but they were just shaking their heads.

"No swimming!" Glimmer yelled, causing a few other campers to look in their direction. "We're practicing today. Only practice!"

Sapphire's jaw dropped. Practicing all day? Sapphire loved to win, and she did think practice was important, but all day seemed like a lot. Sapphire could just see Comet laughing at this turn of events. Not too long ago, Sapphire had tried to convince Comet to stop her other activities and only play hoofball, in order to get ready for a hoofball game!

"Well, uh, we'll see you guys later!" Sparkles said, clearly trying to run away before Glimmer roped them in to help.

"Yeah, bye!" Ray added, and the two hurried out of the mess hall together, leaving Sapphire all alone with Glimmer. Sapphire hoped she would survive the day.

9

The Show Must Go On

The day ended up being just what Glimmer had promised: practice, practice, practice. It was hard work, but Sapphire had to admit that it made her feel better about the routine. She knew just where to put her feet and what to sing. Maybe it was true that practice makes perfect.

After dinner the campers streamed out onto the lawn to watch the performances. Someone had strung up lights on the porch, making it feel even more like a stage. There were streamers and balloons wrapped around the posts. Everything looked so festive!

After admiring the stage—and trying but failing to ignore the nervous butterflies fluttering around in her stomach—Sapphire headed back into the mess hall, where all the performers would wait for their time to shine. Glimmer had rushed off after dinner to get a piece for her costume and had said she would meet Sapphire in the mess hall for a final run-through. But as Sapphire looked around, she couldn't find Glimmer anywhere. The show was going to start any minute. She hoped Glimmer would arrive in time.

Finally Sapphire turned around to see Glimmer walking toward her, but she wasn't in her costume. And she didn't look happy.

"What's wrong, Glimmer?" Sapphire asked. "Are you okay?"

"Well, you're not the real princess, for starters," Glimmer said, stomping her hoof. "And you've been tricking everyone all week!"

Sapphire's heart sank all the way to her hooves. "How

did you find out?" she asked softly, feeling like the whole world was crumbling around her. All her fears seemed to be coming true in this one moment.

"Well, you know nothing about being a princess, which is weird."

Sapphire could only laugh a sad, halfhearted laugh. That was true.

"But I didn't know for sure," Glimmer said. "Not before I went back to the cabin to look for your sunglasses."

Sapphire huffed. "You went through my stall without asking?"

"Well, you pretended to be a princess!"

"Got me there," Sapphire said, feeling guilty.

"Anyway, that's when I found this!" Glimmer presented Comet's note with triumph. As if it were a prize.

Sapphire's jaw dropped. "Oh, Glimmer, I—"

But Glimmer held up a hoof to stop her. "I'll keep your secret, Sapphire."

A rush of happiness came over Sapphire like a wave in the ocean. "Thank you, Glimmer!"

"Well, I'll keep it a secret *if* you tell me who the real princess is."

"No way!" Sapphire was mad that Glimmer would even think she could betray Nellie.

"Fine. If you want it that way," Glimmer said, flipping

her lime-green mane over her shoulder, "I'll tell the whole camp the truth about you. I just signed up for the talent show as a solo act. I'm going to give a dramatic reading." She flashed Comet's note again, looking smug.

Then Glimmer walked away, leaving Sapphire speechless in the middle of the mess hall. Sapphire looked around at the other campers. She couldn't believe everyone around her was still getting ready like everything was normal. As if the world hadn't just totally flipped upside down.

As she was about to crumple on her hooves, Sapphire saw Nellie running toward her with a big smile on her face.

But as she got closer to Sapphire, Nellie's face fell into a frown. "What's wrong?" she asked.

"Everything!" Sapphire said. "Glimmer found my friend Comet's postcard. I'd told her about you and our switch and everything. And Comet's postcard talks about how I'm not a princess and, and, and . . . I'm so sorry, Nellie. I gave away our secret. And now Glimmer is going to tell the whole camp I'm a fraud."

But instead of getting mad, Nellie wrapped her neck around Sapphire in a big hug. "It's okay, it's okay. I'm sorry I ever put you in this position."

Sapphire looked up with tears streaming down her cheeks. "You're not mad at me?"

"Not at all!" Nellie said. "Are you mad at me?"

"No!" Sapphire said, sniffling. "But what are we going to do?"

Nellie smiled. "Well, the show must go on, right?"

10

Like Looking into a Mirror

Sapphire and Nellie waited backstage with the other performers. A few acts had already gone on, and now they were just waiting their turn. Luckily, they'd been able to get a spot ahead of Glimmer.

Nellie had taken off her fake glasses and green wig. And Sapphire had undone her braids so that big curls fell down her back. Both unicorns wore matching sparkly boas.

"It's like looking into a mirror!" Nellie joked.

"What everyone will say?" Sapphire asked. She was nervous about performing and about the campers' reaction to their surprise. But she was also a little excited. It reminded her of the feeling she had before a hoofball game, where everything was unexpected.

A counselor smiled as she made her way to the center of the stage. "Thank you, Beth. That was some of the best juggling I have ever seen! Now please welcome to the stage Nellie and Sapphire!"

Nellie and Sapphire smiled at each other and walked onstage.

The crowd gasped when they saw the fillies together. Sapphire heard unicorns whisper to their neighbors, "Are there two princesses? Is that Nellie?"

Sapphire walked to the middle of the stage and took a deep breath. She was glad Nellie was there with her.

"Perhaps you think you're seeing double," she said to the crowd.

"We're sorry that we tricked you," Nellie added, standing beside her.

"But when we met, we thought fate had brought us together."

"One could see what it was like to be a princess."

"And the other could learn what it was like to be normal."

"But what we didn't expect was that we would both learn what it was like to be a camper!"

They launched into the song they had quickly made up backstage. It was filled with lots of camp jokes and pranks,

and it didn't always rhyme or make sense—*and* they forgot more dance moves than they remembered—but they had fun. And somehow Sapphire wasn't nervous. Not with Nellie by her side.

When they struck their final pose, at first no one said a thing. But then one camper started clapping, then another, and then the whole camp erupted in cheers.

"But which one's which?" someone in the crowd yelled.

"Who is Princess Luna?" another camper called out.

"Any guesses?" Nellie asked.

The crowd fell quiet, as if all the campers were puzzling it over.

Ray spoke up first. "Well, I'm not sure Sapphire is a princess. She reminds me a lot of my older sister, always checking in on people. Sometimes bossing them around. And Princess Luna doesn't have any siblings. I think Nellie was Princess Luna all along!"

Sapphire laughed. She had thought she was keeping her

disguise so well, but it turned out she hadn't fooled anyone after all.

"I think the unicorn formally known as 'Nellie' is the real Princess Luna too!" said Sparkles.

"No way!" another unicorn piped up. "Have you seen Nellie swim? City unicorns can't swim like that!"

The whole audience was talking all at once. Everyone had an opinion! In all the commotion, Sapphire and Nellie snuck offstage.

"Maybe this disguise can remain a secret. It will be one to remember!" Sapphire whispered.

Nellie nodded and smiled. "Thank you, Sapphire," she said. "You've taught me how to make a real friend."

Sapphire could only laugh. "But look at the chaos! Everyone is confused. And probably mad at us."

"I don't think so," Nellie said. "I think it's a camp mystery. And anyway, you taught me how to make a friend because you've been such a good friend to me."

11

Saying Goodbye

Dear Sapphire,

It sounds like you've been a really good friend. And that's always the most important thing. Princess Luna is lucky to have you. ☺

love,

Twilight

The next morning Sapphire packed away all her things. Glimmer, Sparkles, and Ray had packed up all their things too, making the cabin feel empty and sad. It looked lonely without the wet towels hanging out to dry, magazines on the table, or cookie crumbs on the floor.

As Sapphire was taking one last look at her cabin, Glimmer came in. For once she wasn't holding her horn up high. Sapphire went to leave the cabin—she didn't think she could take one more sneer.

"Wait!" Glimmer said, stopping Sapphire in the doorway. "I—uh—came to say . . . Um. Well, I came to say . . ."

Sapphire raised her eyebrows. *What is this about?* she wondered.

"I came to say I'm sorry."

Sapphire's jaw hung open. She hadn't been expecting that.

"It's my fault everyone thought you were a princess in the first place," Glimmer continued. "I told everyone because I wanted everyone to know that a real princess was staying in my cabin."

She looked up at Sapphire. "And I really did think it was true. I mean, you guys are like twins."

Sapphire smiled. "It's okay, Glimmer. I think I get it."

But Glimmer shook her head. "No, I don't think you do. I mean, you naturally have the spotlight. You don't even have to be a princess. I feel like I have to make people pay attention to me. And I was jealous. When I figured out you weren't a princess, I thought I could knock you out of the spotlight. But no one even cared. And no one would believe me anyway. They all have their own theories about who the real princess is!"

Sapphire was surprised. "I was worried everyone was mad at me. Well, everyone but Luna."

"No, no," Glimmer said. "I think everyone likes the mystery. And besides, unicorns just like being around you."

"People like being around you too, Glimmer."

"Really?"

"Yeah! You're fun and smart. You can just be yourself. And maybe be a little nicer."

Glimmer chuckled. "Maybe you're right."

"Glimmer!" a voice called from outside. It sounded like her mom.

"I guess I have to go. See you next summer, Sapphire?"

"Yeah, Glimmer, see you next summer."

Sapphire picked up her bag, with the worn copy of Amelia Hoofheart's autobiography sticking out of the top, and thought about her first day of camp, when she'd worried she had done everything wrong. It turned out that no one felt like they knew how to fit in—not even the camp director's niece. Sapphire had learned that everyone felt nervous and out of place from time to time. Even princesses.

Shamrock's Cursed Hoof

Shamrock felt the spring air brush his cheek as he made his way across the Friendly Fields of Unicorn University. The tall grasses swayed and the few clouds in the sky looked like huge wispy feathers. It was a chilly afternoon and his glasses clouded over as he breathed. He wondered why his lenses always fogged up like that in the cold, and he made a mental to note to look it up in the library later.

Science was always Shamrock's favorite subject at Unicorn University. He loved studying and learning about the ways things worked, even out of the classroom. Potions had to be his favorite class of all, though—he loved following each step in the process to create something magical. But it was a new semester, and instead of Potions class, he had Garden Science. He and his classmates would learn all about magical plants in the Five Kingdoms—and how to grow them! Shamrock was really excited. He had studied the textbook, *Intro to Gardening*, last night and couldn't wait to start studying different plants.

Once he reached the edge of the Friendly Fields, Shamrock found himself at the greenhouse, where Garden Science was held. The structure looked like a house made of big glass windows, even on the roof. Shamrock had read in his textbook that the windows let lots of sunshine in during the day, and then trapped the heat inside after sunset and the air outside cooled at night.

He pushed open the door and felt like he was entering another world. The air was warm and a little sticky, and the whole room smelled like soil. Which made sense as there were plants growing everywhere! Different kinds of plants of every size and color and shape, from a crinkly leafed fern to a bright pink sunflower.

Looking around, Shamrock realized he was the first student there. He always liked to be early on the first day so he could pick his spot and get ready. Searching around the room, he found the perfect table in the corner. It was big—perfect for him and his three best friends—and seemed like the cleanest one, although there were still a few clumps of dirt and empty pots scattered about. Shamrock thought back to his Potions class with its clean tables and shelves of glass bottles with their neat labels. He had to admit, he liked his neat Potions class better. Shamrock liked to be organized, and there was something about this messy greenhouse that made him feel a little squirmy.

As Shamrock settled in, other students started to arrive, and soon the greenhouse was filled with the sounds of unicorns chatting and laughing. Shamrock's friends, Comet, Sapphire, and Twilight came in and sat by him.

"Wow," Twilight said softly. She was gazing around in awe. "This place is magical. I wonder if this is how fairies feel in gardens." With a hoof that was painted bright green, she pointed to some of the bigger plants that hung from the ceiling. The color stood out against her jet-black coat, but blended into the plants all around them. Shamrock wondered if she chose to paint her hooves green just for Garden class.

"I know what you mean!" Comet said. "It feels like we shrunk down to tiny unicorns. A lot of these plants are bigger than us!" Comet whipped her short, cropped hair around to look behind her—almost knocking a potted plant down in the process.

Sapphire reached a bright blue hoof over to catch the pot just in time, and pushed it back on its table.

Sapphire chuckled. "I have no idea what you guys are talking about. But it is cool in here!"

Shamrock was with Sapphire. Comet and Twilight were the artists in their group and sometimes spoke in their own dreamy language. Twilight was a painter, and Comet was an artist with baking pastries.

"I'm pretty excited about this class," Twilight told them. "Growing up on a farm, my parents taught me a lot about gardening, so I feel . . . well, I guess I feel confident?"

Comet laughed. "Yay, Twilight! You totally should. You're the only one in our stable that has kept a plant alive in her stall. You'll be great."

Shamrock nodded in agreement. He was happy to see his friend feeling so confident. Twilight could be shy, and she didn't always believe in herself as much as she should.

"Well, actually . . ." A snow-white unicorn with a red-and-white-striped mane named Peppermint leaned over from her table to theirs. "I heard that the Garden professor is super scary and loves pop quizzes!"

Shamrock smiled. "That would be all right! I've already studied the *Intro to Gardening* book the professor assigned. I would ace any quiz."

"I love that attitude!" The whole class turned to where a dark green unicorn stood in the corner of the greenhouse. Her horn was covered in dirt, and there were leaves tangled in her long green mane. At first glance, she looked like another one of the plants! Shamrock wondered how long she had been there without anyone noticing. He felt embarrassed about bragging now.

The dark green unicorn stepped up to the table and into the light. The whole class could see she was smiling wide. Shamrock thought she seemed friendly, but with all that dirt, Shamrock didn't think she looked much like a scientist. His Potions professor always wore a clean white lab coat.

"I'm Professor Grub," she told them. "And I hope by the end of this class you'll all love the magic of gardening as much as I do."